D0633124

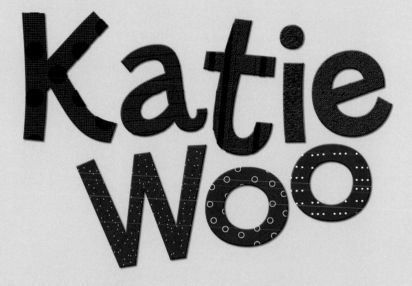

A Happy Day

by Fran Manushkin

illustrated by Tammie Lyon

Picture Window Books
Minneapolis, Minnesota

Katie Woo is published by Picture Window Books, A Capstone Imprint
151 Good Counsel Drive, P.O. Box 669
Mankato, MN 56002
www.capstonepub.com

Library of Congress Cataloging-in-Publication Data
Manushkin, Fran.
    A happy day / by Fran Manushkin; illustrated by Tammie Lyon.
    p. cm. — (Katie Woo)
    ISBN 978-1-4048-5496-3 (library binding)
    [1. Happiness—Fiction. 2. Chinese Americans—Fiction.] I. Lyon, Tammie, ill. II. Title.
PZ7.M3195Hap 2010
[E]—dc22   2009002189

Summary: Katie Woo loves her life and lists the many reasons she is so happy.

Creative Director: Heather Kindseth
Graphic Designer: Emily Harris

Photo Credits
Fran Manushkin, pg. 26
Tammie Lyon, pg. 26

Printed in the United States of America in Stevens Point, Wisconsin.
112014
008606R

 Table of Contents

Chapter 1
Morning Smiles

In the morning, Katie

Woo's kitty, Sweet Pea, wakes

her up with a kiss.

"Your tongue is scratchy,"

Katie tells her cat.

At breakfast, Katie loves

making a milk mustache.

"Your mustache is bigger

and fuzzier than mine!" says

Katie's dad.

"You are both very silly!"

says Katie's mom.

Five days a week, Katie,

Pedro, and JoJo ride to school

together on the bus.

When it is sunny, they feel
cheerful. When it is raining,
they draw funny faces in the
steam on the windows.

"Let's be friends forever!"

Katie tells Pedro and JoJo.

"Okay!" her friends agree.

They give each other a

high five to seal the deal!

At school, Katie likes

passing out the drawing

paper, playing math games,

and writing her name over

and over.

Katie does not like

hearing the chalk squeal on

the blackboard. She is very

happy when it stops!

She is also happy when

the bell rings

for lunch.

Chapter 2
Puddles and Parades

Little things make Katie
Woo happy. Things like
olives and buttons, new
crayons and her fingerprints.

Big things make her
happy too. Things like noisy
drums and high piles of
leaves and loud fireworks on
the Fourth of July.

She loves to hear big

crowds cheering when her

team plays soccer!

Falling down doesn't
make Katie happy. But a
silly Band-Aid makes her feel
a little better.

It is hard to be happy

when it rains.

Wearing her yellow boots

and splashing

in the puddles

makes Katie

feel better.

Katie's mom does not

like to splash in puddles.

Katie can't understand why

not!

Katie doesn't like

watching parades until

her dad lifts her onto his

shoulders.

Then she loves them,

because she can see

everything and wave

at the people.

Katie can't decide what

makes her happier —

tickling someone or being

tickled!

"Spaghetti is the happiest food in the world," Katie tells her mom. "Or maybe ice cream, or maybe birthday cake!"

Katie can't decide.

Bath time is fun when
there are millions of bubbles,
and Katie can wear a crown
of them on her head.

Chapter 3
A Happy Ending

During the day, Katie

feels happy seeing the sun

shining on the lake.

At night, the moon shines into Katie's room. There are shooting stars to wish on.

Spending all day with her
family and friends always
makes Katie feel great!

It's also great when each
day ends the same way it
began.

"Your kiss is scratchy,
Sweet Pea," says Katie Woo.
"But it makes me happy!"

About the Author

Fran Manushkin is the author of many popular picture books, including *How Mama Brought the Spring; Baby, Come Out!; Latkes and Applesauce: A Hanukkah Story;* and *The Tushy Book.* There is a real Katie Woo — she's Fran's great-niece — but she never gets in half the trouble of the Katie Woo in the books. Fran writes on her beloved Mac computer in New York City, without the help of her two naughty cats, Cookie and Goldy.

About the Illustrator

Tammie Lyon began her love for drawing at a young age while sitting at the kitchen table with her dad. She continued her love of art and eventually attended the Columbus College of Art and Design, where she earned a bachelors degree in fine art. After a brief career as a professional ballet dancer, she decided to devote herself full time to illustration. Today she lives with her husband, Lee, in Cincinnati, Ohio. Her dogs, Gus and Dudley, keep her company as she works in her studio.

 Glossary

chalk (CHAWK)—a stick of soft, white rock that is used to write on blackboards

fuzzier (FUHZ-ee-er)—something that looks like it is covered with more fuzz than something else

mustache (MUHSS-tash)—the hair that grows on a person's upper lip

scratchy (SKRACH-ee)—rough and itchy

spaghetti (spuh-GET-ee)—long, thin strands of pasta made of flour and water and cooked by boiling

tongue (TUHNG)—the movable muscle in the mouth that is used to taste and talk

Discussion Questions

1. Katie wakes up happy in the morning. Some people do not like mornings. They wake up a little crabby. Are you happy or crabby in the morning?

2. The book lists some of Katie's favorite things at school. What are your favorite parts of school?

3. When Katie falls down, she feels sad. But a Band-Aid makes her feel better. What makes you feel better when you are sad?

Writing Prompts

1. Katie rides the bus to school with her friends. How do you get to school? What do you like about the daily trip? Write a paragraph about it.

2. Katie cannot decide what the happiest food is. What do you think the happiest food is? Draw a picture of the happiest food and write a sentence to describe it.

3. Katie likes to end her day with a kiss from Sweet Pea. What sort of things do you do at the end of the day? Do you brush your teeth? Read a story? Write the steps down in order.

Having Fun with Katie Woo

In *A Happy Day*, we find out all the things that make Katie happy. Think about what makes you happy, and make a happiness mobile.

What you need:

- construction paper
- scissors
- a paper punch
- yarn
- markers
- a hanger
- old magazines or photos and glue, optional

What to do:

1. Draw five to ten various shapes — like triangles, circles, and squares — on the construction paper. Make them as big as your hand. Next, carefully cut them out and punch a hole in each. (If you need help, ask a grown-up.)

2. On each shape, write down something that makes you happy. If you want, you can also show a picture of each thing. Use photos or look through old magazines for pictures. Glue them onto your shapes.

3. Cut a piece of yarn for each shape. They should be a range of lengths, from twelve to twenty inches. Tie one end of each piece to a shape. Tie the other end to the hanger.

Once all your shapes are tied to the hanger, your mobile is finished! Ask a grown-up to hang it up, and watch your happy things spin.